Autumn Leaves

Written by Virginia Ferguson and Peter Durkin

Illustrated by Susan Swan

Leaves in my sleeves,
Leaves in my hair,
Autumn is leaving leaves everywhere.

2

Leaves in my dress,
Leaves in my shirt,
Autumn is throwing leaves in the dirt.

4

Leaves when it rains,
Leaves when it blows,
Autumn leaves leaves wherever it goes.

5

Leaves in the air,
Leaves on the ground
Autumn paints leaves with never a sound.

Leaves in my ears,
Leaves in my eyes,
Autumn gives trees a winter surprise.

Leaves in my sleeves,
Leaves in my hair,
Autumn is leaving leaves everywhere!

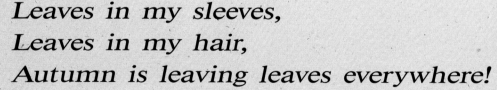